Hoothoot's Haunted Forest

#13

POKÉMON junior

Adapted by Tracey West

SCHOLASTIC INC.
New York Toronto London Auckland Sydney
Mexico City New Delhi Hong Kong Buenos Aires

No part of this publication may be reproduced in whole or in part, or stored in a retrieval system, or transmitted in any form or by any means, electronic, mechanical, photocopying, recording, or otherwise, without written permission of the publisher. For information regarding permission, write to Scholastic Inc., Attention: Permissions Department, 555 Broadway, New York, NY 10012.

ISBN 0-439-32066-6

© 1995-2001 Nintendo, CREATURES, GAME FREAK.

TM & ® are trademarks of Nintendo.

© 2001 Nintendo.

Published by Scholastic Inc. All rights reserved.
SCHOLASTIC and associated logos are trademarks and/or registered trademarks of Scholastic Inc.

Designed by Carisa Swenson

12   7 8 9/0

Printed in the U.S.A.
First Scholastic printing, September 2001

CHAPTER ONE

Lost!

"I think we are lost," said Misty.

"Pika!" agreed Pikachu.

Pikachu was walking through
the woods with Misty, Brock, and
Ash, its trainer. The friends were
on a journey to become great
Pokémon trainers. Usually, they
had a good time. But sometimes

things went wrong. Like now.

It was getting late. And dark. The woods looked very spooky.

Pikachu looked up at Ash. "No worries," Ash said. "We will be through this forest soon."

Ash ran ahead. Pikachu smiled. If Ash was not worried, then Pikachu would not worry, either.

The friends walked and walked. Then Pikachu heard something.

Whoo hoo hoo!

"Do not kid around, Brock," Misty said.

"It wasn't me," Brock said.

Whooooooooo! They heard the creepy sound again.

"Who is it?" Ash asked.

Whoo hoo hoo! The sound got louder.

Suddenly, a spooky face formed on a tree trunk.

"Help!" Ash cried.

CHAPTER TWO

Help from Gary

Pikachu wanted to help Ash. It wanted to give the scary tree a Thundershock. But it was so scared! It could not move.

Then a Pokémon came out of the trees. It had a round body. It had brown feathers and a yellow beak. It hopped on one leg.

A red light came out of the Pokémon's eyes. The light shone on the tree.

The scary face vanished. Now the tree looked like a normal tree.

A tall boy came out of the trees next. It was Gary, Ash's rival. Gary was always one step ahead of Ash.

"Well done, Hoothoot," said Gary. He patted the Pokémon on the head.

Ash took out his pocket computer, Dexter. "Tell me about Hoothoot," Ash said.

"Hoothoot, the Owl Pokémon," Dexter said. "It always stands on one leg. It can see clearly, even in the darkest night."

"The only way to get through this forest is with a Hoothoot," Gary said. "You should know that, Ash."

Ash frowned. Pikachu knew that Gary could be very mean. But right now Ash needed his help.

"Why do we need a Hoothoot?" Ash asked him.

"What you saw was an illusion," Gary said. "It was not real. Hoothoot can spot the illusions. It can make them vanish."

"Where can we get one?" Ash asked.

Gary laughed. "That is for you to figure out," he said. Then Gary and the Hoothoot walked away.

Ash turned to his friends.

"I will get us out of this forest," he said. "I will get us a Hoothoot!"

CHAPTER THREE

Follow That Hoothoot!

"Hoothoot! Come out, Hoothoot!" Ash called out.

Ash climbed up a tree to look for a Hoothoot. Pikachu stayed on the ground with the others.

Brock took out some of his Pokémon food. "I have a treat for you, Hoothoot," Brock said.

But no Hoothoot came.

Then Pikachu saw something.

A Hoothoot hopped up behind Misty!

Misty did not see it. She took a step. Hoothoot hopped after her.

Misty took another step.

Hoothoot hopped again. It really seemed to like Misty.

Ash saw the Hoothoot. He climbed down from the tree.

"Over here, Hoothoot," Ash said.

Hoothoot stopped. Then it hopped onto Ash's head! It pecked at Ash with its sharp beak.

"Hey!" Ash cried.

Pikachu ran to help Ash. But Hoothoot moved fast. It jumped off Ash's head. Then it ran into the woods.

"Come back!" Ash yelled. Ash, Pikachu, Misty, and Brock ran after Hoothoot.

They followed Hoothoot to a clearing. A stone arch rose up in

front of them. Hoothoot ran
through the arch.

"It is moving too fast," Ash said.
"We have to catch it or we will
never get out of these woods.
Pikachu, use Thundershock!"

"Pika!" said Pikachu.

Pikachu was happy to help. It
tried to catch up with Hoothoot.

But Hoothoot turned around. It
flew onto Ash's head again.

Pikachu could not shock
Hoothoot now. Ash might get
hurt!

Hoothoot pecked and pecked at

Ash's head again.

"Ouch!" Ash yelled.

Then they heard an angry voice. "What are you doing?"

CHAPTER FOUR

A Hoothoot To Guide Them

A woman walked through the arch. She was very old.

"Watch out," Brock said. "She may be an illusion."

"I am no illusion," the woman snapped. "I am Agatha. I rent Hoothoot to people who pass through this forest. Come with me, I will tell you all about it."

Agatha led them to a table in her small wooden house.

"There are strange Pokémon in these woods," Agatha explained.

"Is that what causes these illu-sions?" Ash asked.

Agatha nodded. "Yes. Hoothoot can see through the illusions."

"We would like to rent a Hoothoot," Ash said. "We need to get through these woods tonight."

Agatha scratched her chin. "Hmm. I would like to. But the Hoothoot you found in the forest

is the only one I have left. It is not a very good guide."

"What do you mean?" asked Misty.

"The last trainer who rented it got lost for three days," said Agatha. "I am sorry. The rest of my Hoothoot will be back tomorrow."

"We can't wait," Ash said. "Gary will get too far ahead of us." He picked up Hoothoot. "I think this Hoothoot can do it. That other trainer got lost, but I won't. What do you say, Hoothoot?"

Hoothoot wriggled out of Ash's arms. It jumped into Misty's lap.

Agatha grinned. "I forgot to tell you. This Hoothoot likes pretty girls."

"Pretty girls? Where?" Ash asked. Misty scowled at him.

"If Hoothoot likes Misty, then

maybe it will go with us," Brock said.

"Is that right, Hoothoot?" Ash asked. "Will you do it?"

"Hoot! Hoot!" Hoothoot said. *Yes! I will try.*

"All right!" Ash said. "Then let's go back to the woods."

Pikachu looked into the woods. The sky was black now. The woods looked spookier than ever.

Could they trust the Pokémon to get them through the forest safely? There was only one way to find out!

CHAPTER FIVE

Strange Lights

They left Agatha's house and walked back into the forest. Pikachu stayed close to Ash.

For a while, everything was fine. Then Hoothoot began to shake. It flapped its wings.

"What's the matter, Hoothoot?" Misty asked.

Just then, a glowing ball of yellow light appeared in the air. Then another. And another.

The balls of light swirled in the air. They swooped down and tried to hit Ash, Misty, and Brock. The friends ducked.

"They must be illusions, too," said Brock.

"Help us, Hoothoot!" Ash said.

But Hoothoot began to run away.

"Please, Hoothoot?" Misty asked.

Hoothoot stopped. It turned and faced the balls of light. Red beams came out of Hoothoot's eyes. The beams hit the balls of light. Nothing happened.

"Try harder, Hoothoot!" Ash said.

But Hoothoot was too afraid.

The balls of light danced in the air. They came together. They formed a face. A scary face with big eyes and a wide mouth.

The same face from the tree! *Whoooooo!* it moaned.

CHAPTER SIX

> **More Trouble**

"Hoot Hoot!" Hoothoot screamed and ran away from the face.

Without Hoothoot to help them, Pikachu did not know how to fight the illusion. It was the scariest thing Pikachu had ever seen!

Ash, Misty, and Brock ran away,

too. Pikachu ran right with them.

Soon they were out of breath. Pikachu looked behind them.

The face was gone.

Ash scolded Hoothoot. "Why did you run away?"

"Hoot hoot," said Hoothoot sadly. It looked at its feet.

"Agatha said this Hoothoot was not a good guide," Misty said.

Ash picked up Hoothoot. "I don't care what Agatha says. I believe in you," he said. "You have to try. You have to!"

Hoothoot looked into Ash's

eyes. Pikachu watched. Was
Hoothoot going to listen to Ash?

Not yet. Hoothoot jumped out
of Ash's arms. It hopped over to
Misty.

Misty knelt down next to
Hoothoot. "Don't you want to be a
forest guide, like the other

Hoothoot?" Misty asked.

Hoothoot nodded.

"Then guide us through these woods," Misty said. "We can do it together."

"Hoot! Hoot!" Hoothoot said. *I will do it for you, Misty.*

Ash frowned. Pikachu knew that Ash wanted to train Hoothoot by himself.

Then a rope swooped down from the sky. It wrapped around Pikachu's body.

"Pika!" Pikachu screamed.

CHAPTER SEVEN

Team Rocket!

Pikachu looked up. A boy, a
girl, and a white Pokémon were
crouched in the tree branches. It
was Jessie, James, and Meowth.
These three Pokémon thieves
were known as Team Rocket.

Team Rocket was always
causing trouble. And they were

26

always trying to steal Pikachu.
Today, Jessie and James had a
giant fishing pole. They were using
it to reel in Pikachu.

Ash tried to save Pikachu. He
grabbed onto his Pokémon. But
Jessie and James swung the rope.

Ash crashed into a tree.

Jessie and James scooped up Pikachu. They stuffed it into a box.

"Nice catch," Meowth told Jessie and James. Then Meowth grinned. "I hope you like this electric-proof box, Pikachu!"

Pikachu was so angry. Now it could not use its electric attacks to escape.

Jessie, James, and Meowth jumped into a boat. The boat was attached to ropes. The ropes stretched from tree to tree.

Team Rocket pulled on the ropes. The boat creaked as it moved along the ropes.

Then, *snap!* The ropes broke. The boat fell to the ground.

Ash moved fast. He caught Pikachu's box. Then he set his Pokémon free.

"Pika!" said Pikachu. *Thanks, Ash.*

But Team Rocket was not finished. Jessie and James each held out a Poké Ball.

"You are asking for it," Jessie said angrily. "Let's battle!"

CHAPTER EIGHT

Ash, Ash, Everywhere!

Jessie and James threw their Poké Balls. Arbok flew out of one ball. The cobra Pokémon had a long, purple body.

Victreebel flew out of another ball. The yellow Pokémon looked like a big flower bell. It quickly swallowed James.

30

James kicked his legs. "Do not attack *me*! Attack *them*," James said.

Pikachu was not afraid. It knew it could take on Arbok and Victreebel.

Ash threw out a Poké Ball, too. Out popped Bulbasaur, a blue-green Pokémon. A big plant bulb sat on its back.

With Bulbasaur's help, Pikachu knew they could get rid of Team Rocket. Pikachu got ready to fight.

Then a strange fog floated

through the air. Hoothoot jumped up and down.

The fog vanished. Then Pikachu saw something strange. A Dragonite was walking through the trees. The big orange Pokémon had white wings on its back.

Team Rocket got excited.

"What is a rare Pokémon like that doing here?" asked James.

"Who cares?" said Meowth. "Let's catch it!"

Team Rocket ran off after the Dragonite.

"They must be seeing an illusion," Brock said.

Pikachu smiled. The illusions were spooky. But at least this one took care of Team Rocket.

"Hoot! Hoot!" Hoothoot flapped its wings again.

It must be another illusion, Pikachu thought.

Pikachu was right. A double of Ash appeared next to Pikachu's trainer. Pikachu rubbed its eyes. *Two Ashes?*

Then another Ash appeared. And another.

Soon there were Ashes every-
where!

CHAPTER NINE

Misty Bugs Out

"Pikachu, it's me! I am the real Ash!" said one of the boys.

"No, it is me!" said another.

"No, I am the real one!" said another.

"Tell them, Pikachu!"

Pikachu looked from one Ash to another. One of them was the real

Ash. The rest were fakes. But which one was real?

Pikachu's head hurt. They all looked alike. Then Pikachu had an idea.

"Pikachuuuuuuuuuuuu!" Pikachu blasted all the boys with an electric shock.

The fake boys vanished. Only one Ash remained. He looked frazzled, but he was all right.

"Uh, thanks Pikachu," said Ash.

"Pika!" said Pikachu. *No problem!*

Pikachu felt proud. It took care

of the illusions. Maybe now they could get through the forest. They did not need Hoothoot.

Suddenly, Misty screamed.

Pikachu looked. Bug Pokémon surrounded Misty. There was a green Caterpie. A Beedrill with sharp stingers. A Venomoth with poison fangs. A Metapod with a hard shell. And a crawly brown Weedle.

"Help!" Misty yelled.

CHAPTER TEN

Hoothoot Saves the Day

"Hang in there, Misty," Brock said. "It is just an illusion."

"That is easy for you to say!" Misty shot back. She hugged Togepi tightly.

Usually Misty was very brave. But she had one weakness. She disliked Bug Pokémon!

Hoothoot was afraid of the Bug Pokémon, too. It started to run away. Ash grabbed it.

"You cannot leave Misty," Ash said. "You are the only one that can save her. You can do it, Hoothoot."

Hoothoot nodded. Pikachu thought it looked different from before. It looked brave.

It aimed its red eyes at the Bug Pokémon.

A powerful red beam shot out of Hoothoot's eyes. The beam hit the Bug Pokémon. This time it

worked! The Bug Pokémon all vanished.

"Good job, Hoothoot," said Ash.

"*Pika!*" said Pikachu. *You rule!*

"*Hoot hoot. Hoot!*" said Hoothoot. *I will find out who is making these illusions.*

Hoothoot shone a red beam into the trees. The beam seemed to light up the whole forest.

Pikachu gasped. Before, the trees looked empty. But Hoot-hoot's red beam revealed Ghost Pokémon in the trees!

There were scary-looking gray

40

Haunter with big claws. There
were tough-looking Gengar with
creepy orange eyes. Pikachu
could not believe it.

"Aha," said Brock. "So the
Ghost Pokémon
were behind those
illusions."
The Ghost Pokémon
cackled. They smiled mean
smiles.

"Bulbasaur,
Vine Whip!"
Ash called
out.

Two green vines lashed out of Bulbasaur's plant bulb. The vines reached up and knocked the Ghost Pokémon out of the trees.

"Pikachu, Thunderbolt!" Ash shouted.

"Pikachuuuuuu!" Pikachu let loose with a sizzling Thunderbolt. The blast shocked the Ghost Pokémon as they fell to the ground.

The Ghost Pokémon did not stay to fight. They flew away as fast as they could.

"We did it!" Ash cried.

CHAPTER ELEVEN

Morning at Last

Ash picked up Hoothoot. "Thanks, Hoothoot. You finally listened to me," he said.

Hoothoot jumped on Ash's head. Then it started pecking him!

Misty laughed. "I don't think you trained Hoothoot, Ash. I think

Hoothoot just wanted to help me. Right?"

"Hoot!" said Hoothoot. *Right, Misty.*

Ash gave in. "I guess it does not matter why you did it, Hoothoot. I am just glad that you helped us."

"Pikachu!" said Pikachu. *You can say that again.*

But they were not out of the woods yet. The friends kept walking. Hoothoot led the way.

Soon the sun rose over the treetops. Hoothoot led them to a big stone arch. It looked just like

the arch they had seen earlier.

Then a very small, very old woman walked up to them. She looked just like Agatha!

"Oh, no!" said Brock. "It is another illusion."

"Don't be silly," said the woman. "I am Hagatha. Agatha is my twin sister. You are at the other end of the forest."

"We made it," said Misty.

"I told you I would get us through the forest," said Ash.

Misty and Brock groaned.

Pikachu laughed. The long

night was over.

It felt great to be out of those
spooky woods!